TABLE OF CONTENTS

CHAPTER ONE

Being sixteen should be a good time for me, growing up in the streets of Brooklyn; life is never usually what it appears to be. The youngest of eight and in private school, trying to make all good grades beginning a cheerleader and getting straight A's. But you never know when your life is going to change for the better or the worst, you never know when you go to sleep and wake up tomorrow just might be your last day on earth. My family had shelter me from what these mean streets held.

I was never allowed to hang around with the people in my hood, too many teenage pregnancies and my mom thought they were up to no good. So, my family thought by sending me to private school away from my neighborhood would be good for me, but if they only knew. Things were going good for me; I remember it like it was yesterday, when I met this guy on my way to school. I remember my family telling me never talk to anyone that lives in your hood, so I thought it was cool. I weighed out my options, one he is an older guy and two he is not from my hood.

Once we started talking, it was something about him that caught my attention, those hazels eyes and his caramel complexion. The way he dressed and smelled, the way he spoke; man, I was mesmerized by his sweet seductive voice. We could have talked all day with a little laughing and a little friendly play, then he gave me his number and told me to call him then I walked away. I was thinking about him all day and night. I really wanted to call but I did not want to look or sound too desperate, so I did not call at all.

Days and weeks went by and I had not called him. One Friday I was on my way to school and I heard someone calling my name.

I turned around and to my surprise it was him, the guy with the seductive voice that had me mesmerize. I played it off like I did not know who he was. He said "hi, I know you remember me, I was waiting for that call". My reply was "oh I just got caught up with a lot of things", not knowing that this day would be the day that my life was going to change.

He asked me out on a date. I was reluctant to say yes, but the way his eyes pierced and penetrated my body and it made me feel like he could see straight throw my soul. And The way his mouth moved and how he licked his lips I kept fantasizing. I knew I should not be thinking that way, but he had me hypnotize, then I said yes. I could not let my family know because he was an older guy and I knew that they will not accept that at all.

That night I waited for my family to go to bed. I snuck out of the house to meet him. He picked me up around the corner instead of in front of my house. I knew my nosey neighbor Mrs. Jenkins would be looking out, and I could not afford for her to see me and tell my mom.

I knew if I should get caught, what the price I would have to pay. So, I took a chance and told him I had to be home before the break of day. We went out to eat and talked all night long. Telling each other what our likes and dislikes is and even our favorite songs. I kept it one hundred with him, all night I kept telling myself this guy is the one for me.

Days, weeks and months went by. I was now his woman and he was my man. I was always a good judge of character but damn he had me fooled. He was my first and he made love to me, I have to admitted it, he had me weak in the knees. The pleasure he gave me had me exploding like a stick of dynamite.

CHAPTER TWO

He did things to me sexually I never imaged. He blew my mind and had me coming back, wanting more and more, but lately I have been noticing a change in him. staying out late, making all types of excuses and frequents calls. I stopped asking questions and getting no answers.

So, I decided when he goes out tonight, I will start my search through his house, to figure out what is going on with him. I knew that he was not going to be home until 10pm. So, this gave me enough time to start doing some investigation. Damn his house was so big. I did not know where to start,

I kept telling myself remember you have only until ten o'clock". The first place I started was the bedroom because this was our love nest. I started opening draws and closets. Damn I turned that room upside down. I opened a closet that he had in the back and walked inside and to my surprise, I saw a big safe, a bunch of guns and ammunitions on the floor.

It looked like he was preparing to go to war. I kept asking myself what in the hell I done got myself into. Being with this guy so long and not knowing what he does for a living. I always assumed he worked in a bank, with his fancy house, cars and all those expensive suits. What is a Brooklyn girl like me supposed to think?

Should I pack up my clothes and hide out for a bit? Or should I just act like I do not know shit? Damn, I heard someone coming in the door. I started cleaning up my mess like I had superpowers. When he came in, I acted like nothing ever happened. I could not tell him what I knew, because I could have been sleeping with the enemy and I did not know what he would do to me had he knew what I know.

CHAPTER THREE

So, I knew I had to keep everything I know on the down low. It had me thinking that this relationship is built on lies. I wondered what else he was hiding from me. I could not sleep at all thinking about what I had discovered. Sometimes people say, "don't go looking for things because you don't want to find out the answer."

I thought to myself maybe I should not search anymore, but I was dying to know what I got myself involved in by being with him and being his woman. I could not even go to my family about this because they would beat my ass. One they do not know I am dating this older man and two I have been lying saying that I am at a friend house. What am I going to do? So, I kept my mouth shut and continued to go to school like nothing was wrong.

Lately I have noticed every morning I see this black Sedan following me on my way to school. Who could it be? No one in this neighborhood knows about me I thought to myself. My man called me about 2:15 in the afternoon, he told me he is on his way to pick me up. I told him I thought someone had been following me. He brushed it off and kept telling me it is all in my head.

He told me that night we were going out and he had some people that he would like for me to meet. I wore a low-cut black fitting dress with a split above my thigh and a pair of silver 6 ½ inch stilettos. When we arrived at my surprise there were hundreds of people and guards surrounding the place from front to back. You would have thought that the president was in town, because everyone was all suited up and dressed in all black. When our car approached the scene, I noticed everyone paused, you could have heard a pin drop in there,

CHAPTER FOUR

They started bowing their heads to him. I did not know what that was all about. I just smiled and proceeded to the house. When we went inside people was lined up on both sides, clearing the path for us to go through. A table was placed in the center of the floor for us to sit.

I thought that was kind of strange because we were the only ones sitting there. So, they all stood up until we took our seat. My inner voice was saying "what the hell is going on? Is this a cult? Are they going to sacrifice me?" Because I realized I was the only one that I did not know anyone there. My man told everyone to take their seats and they began to sit down.

I looked at him with such a fright on my face, wondering what kind of control he has over these people for them to be listening to him. So, he raised his glass and told everyone I like to make an announcement. He told me to stand up and I did not say a word. What came out of his mouth I thought I did not hear him clear, he said this is my Queen and respect her as such. I thought that was a bit too much, not knowing what he meant when he said" Queen". I had no clue what Queen was in their circle. Drug Queen Pin and he is the King.

On my way home, I could not even speak, just thinking about what just transpired that night. I am only sixteen and dating a drug lord! I am in too deep. The ride home was the longest ride ever. My heart was beating so loud you can hear it through my chest. He leaned over and kiss me so passionately and said "you're mines forever. I was trying to figure out just what and the hell he meant by that because, the look he had in his eyes I never seen it before.

When we arrived home, I went upstairs to run a hot bath and lit some scented candles. Before I could do anything, he started taking off my clothes, kissing and caressing my body. He knows what that does to me. Is he trying to tame me with sex? I thought, but the whole time he was giving me pleasure I could not stop thinking about what happened.

I want to be with him, but everyone knows what this type of lifestyle brings, prison or death. The next morning around 3 A.M I kept hearing his phone going off, but he was still asleep. The phone stopped ringing and they left a voice message. So, I decided to play it. The message said "there will be a shipment coming in so let us set up a meeting today at 6:30 P.M. If you like what is on the table, we can negotiate a price."

I snuck back into bed before he realizes that I was gone. When I woke up, I saw that he was checking his voice messages not knowing that I had heard it already. So, he looked over at me and said "Babe I have a business meeting to go to tonight and I need for you to go with me. My inner voice is saying "is he fucking kidding me? He is getting ready to go and do some illegal shit and have me as an accessory, so if he gets caught, I am going down too.

But I had no choice in this matter but to say yes, because I remembered that he had all those guns in the backroom closet. Shit I am not stupid. Later, that evening I heard my man on the phone calling Tony, he is one of his home boys I met back then when we first hooked up. Then he said we have a meeting tonight so get your men; I will be driving a white Bentley so tell the boys to bring their tools.

I was trying to figure out what did he mean by bring your tools? He looks over at me and smile. We arrived at the meeting I noticed that I was the only woman there and second why was everyone strapped if this was going to be a business meeting. I was getting extremely nervous I wanted to run out of there screaming for my life, but I started shaking and sweating. My man whom they call Lucky grabbed a hold of my hand and looked at me and said baby calm down. I would never let no one harm you remember you are mines and you are my queen.

CHAPTER FIVE

When he said that I got a flash back of what happened last night when he told his people I am his queen and respect me as such. Oh, hell no, why does he keep saying that is this man going to kill me if I decide to leave him, or am I am making too much out of this? I wonder. As we approach the group of men, Lucky businessman looks over at me and said who is this sweet young thing? and what is she to you Lucky? Lucky looked over at me and said my Queen and smiled. I said to myself why and the hell would he say that to him because if shit do not go right, they are going to come looking for me. So, I smiled and excused myself and ask where the ladies' room was. Lucky looked over at his right-hand man and said he will take you. As I approached the bathroom I went inside to freshen up and all I heard was a loud sound of rounds going off. I dropped to the floor and Tony rushed into the bathroom, grabbed me and said hurry we got to go. I was scared out of my mind. What and the hell just happened? I was running for dear life trying to figure out where Lucky was. Tony pushed me in the car and drove off. I was screaming stop where's Lucky? he told me to take you home.

The whole ride I was crying and saying what happened? what happen? he said you will be safe? I must get back to Lucky. As we approached the house there were four cars lined up in the driveway and I looked over at Tony to get some kind of reaction from him. He just told me to go inside and said that there will be nine armed guards, guarding me until further notice from the boss. When I went inside there were guards posted all through the house. I was so frightened I didn't know what to do, so I went in the bedroom and locked the door trying to figure out how am I'm going to get out of this house because I can hear one of the guards outside my bedroom door.

I started to have a panic attack because I realized if shit goes down, I am the only one not strapped. So, I remembered the guns inside the closet, so I opened the door and went inside and picked up a magnum with a few rounds by my side, I kept one round in the chamber if I had to bust it quick. I never shot off a gun before, but I kept my back against the closet door preparing myself for anything. I could not sleep all night waiting for my man to call not knowing if he was ok, that was the hardest part. Around 3am there was knock on the door. I was so afraid to open it. I said who is it? with the gun in my hand ready to shoot. A voice answered it is Lucky.

So, I jumped up and ran to the door Lucky was sweating like he just did ten laps around the park with blood on his clothes and looking dazed and confused. I never seen him like this before. I was so happy to see him. I said Babe are you alright? what and the hell happen back there? I was so worried about you when I was running for my life. He said do not worry about it, I have it all under control as he proceeded to take off his bloody clothes. I noticed he pulled a gun from his hip and laid it beside the bed. He headed towards the bathroom to wash the blood off him he called for me take a shower with him. As the tears ran down my cheek, I put my head on his chest. He held me tightly and kissed me on my head, as he carried me out of the shower. He laid me on the bed as we began to make love and he whispered in my ear I would die for you.

I never loved anyone like this before until I met you. Just hearing those words from his mouth, it felt like my heart just stopped. The saying must be true, good sex makes a person speak their mind. I looked him in his beautiful hazel eyes and told him I love you too, damn I am whipped. With all this crazy shit going on, a sane girl would have hauled ass out of there.

CHAPTER SIX

But like they say love make you do crazy things. While Lucky begins to fall asleep, holding me tight, I am lying in his arms just thinking about what if he would have been killed back there? Would I be marked for death; remember he had announced me as his Queen. I am living a double life and I am only sixteen. What would my family think of the path I have chosen? I know they would maybe disown me because I had been warned about these mean streets may hold. The next morning, I woke up, Lucky was steering at me and said we need to talk. I could just imagine what he was about to say.

Do I really want to know what happened last night? I took a deep breath and tried to prepare myself for what comes next? He sat beside me and caressed my face and said baby girl I killed a man last night, please hear me out and do not say a word until I am finished. I always told you I would not let anyone hurt you and I would kill and die for you and believe me I mean every word I say. Last night shit just got out of control the kilos of drugs they tried to sell us the shit was no good when we tested it. He tried to play me for a fool. I warned him before because he sold me some bad product 3 weeks ago and I told him don't let this happened again and don't waste my time because the outcome won't be good when you have 100,000 on the table.

I knew if I told you from the beginning that I was a drug lord which included money laundering, drug trafficking and firearm deals which also leads to murder, that you wouldn't have talked to me or gave me second look, or even be my woman, that's why I tried to keep this from you. When you started asking question, I did not want to tell you babe. I did not want to lose you. I am in deep into this relationship. So, that is why I introduced you to my world and made it official by letting everyone know that you are my Queen. Now that I have told you are you going to still be my Queen would you stand by my side; would you ride or die for me. I was speechless. I thought I just died and went straight to hell. The look on my face was priceless, it felt like my life just flashed right before my eyes and I could not catch up to it fast enough.

I was saying to myself oh damn now that he told me I am an accessory to murder, drug trafficking and firearm deals. One I was there when it went down, and two Lucky introduced me as the Queen pin and my fingerprints are at the scene when I went to the bathroom. These things are going through my head, for this type of shit I could get life. A few minutes went by Lucky came back upstairs and said baby girl come on we must go, so I jumped out of the bed and started to put on my clothes. My heart was racing. I did not know what in the hell was going on. He said were going for a ride.

I was saying to myself oh hell no not again when he took me for a ride the first time all hell broke loose. I was running for my damn life; this seems like Deja vu all over again. When I arrived downstairs, I noticed his guards were waiting. As I approached the car, I noticed Lucky was not driving, it was Tony. I got into the back seat and Lucky was inside already he looked at me and smiled. I was wondering what and the hell is he smiling about this shit done got really serious. I was so clueless about what was going on. So, I did not say a word the whole ride.

I noticed that we were leaving Brooklyn and ended up in Connecticut to meet with Lucky's brother Rick. I never met him before, but I was always told never attempt to betray him because the last person who did was never seen again. I did not know how true that statement was, but I am was not trying to find out. We finally arrived but to me it felt like an eternity. We approached the entrance of a black gate, where you had to be buzzed inside. There were guards all around and the house was miles away you could not walk to the house on foot it was so far away. I thought why in the hell would you want to live so far back in the woods?

Oh, my guess you have something to hide. I scoped the place out before I enter inside. There were so many rooms as far as the eyes can see and so many places to hide. I said to myself this time if shit goes down, I am going to be the first one to flee. I learned my lesson believe me.

I learned to always be aware of your surrounding and never take your eyes off anyone, especially the ones that you do not know. Lucky was holding my hand so tight he must of new that I was scared being in a strange place and my family did not know I was there. Rick came out of know where, he must have a secret entrance that I did not see. He approaches us from behind and asks Lucky who is this pretty thing I see, Lucky replied this is my queen Alisha; oh, you must really be into her. He replied you never brought anyone here before, you must trust her more than life itself and to bring her around into this lifestyle do she know what we do Lucky.

Lucky answered yes, I announced to everyone that she is my Queen, but Lucky she so young Rick said. Rick age is nothing but a number, I love her was Lucky's response. I would kill for her I would die for her. Damn when he said that to him, I had to take a deep breath. I think I held it in for so long I almost passed out. So, Rick turned around to me you heard what my brother said do you feel the same way? if you betray my brother even though I know he love you, I'll kill you.

When he said that, I got quiet. I looked at Lucky and I was saying to myself oh know the fuck he did not say that shit to me, now before I answered his question, I thought hard about what I was going to say. I said to myself this is my enemy and if shit goes down, he would be the first one I will kill. I turned around and looked Rick dead in his eyes, with blood in my eyes and said yes, I do love Lucky I would die for him and I would kill anyone who comes between Lucky and I. Lucky smiled. So, Rick said I heard what went down the other night between you and the Deserta family.

CHAPTER SEVEN

Lucky replied I told that piece of shit if he sells me another bad batch of product that he would not like the result. Damn Lucky Rick replied this shit is bad, you know that you done started and all-out war between the two families. Why didn't you come to me and let me handle it? You know everyone is marked for death now. Hold up wait a minute what he means by everyone shit, I saying to myself hell I just got in this relationship. He looks at Lucky and said Alisha is too, remember you announced her as your Queen, was she there when the gun fight went down, Lucky replied yes. Now we all are going to have to watch our backs and be prepared for war you need to keep her with guards at all times. She needs to learn how to protect herself at all cost.

Now I am standing there, when Rick said that I see my life flash right before my eyes. I look at Lucky and said what about my family what is going to happen to them. He said do not worry babe I got it covered. The soldiers are already staked out by your house. What? Yeah, they been watching your family ever since that shit went down the other night, so Lucky where do we go from here. I am going to teach you the business and you must learn it fast and follow everything step by step. Your life and my life plus your family life depend on everything I teach you from this day on. If you fuck up, we are all dead.

CHAPTER EIGHT

You see the way you look and so young no one would ever suspect you can be so dangerous. You will learn how to test the product, make deals, sell guns, launder money and finally if shit goes down you will have to kill or be killed, because if anything should ever happen to me you will have to take over my Queen and you will have to run it with an iron fist don't trust no one. Trust only yourself and always keep your friends close but your enemies closer, you hear me? Yes, I do. That night seemed like it was going on forever. I was thinking I cannot do this but since I was doing adult things this is the ultimate price I have to pay damn, I am holding everyone life in my hands, I am in too deep.

All night long Lucky and Rick was teaching me everything I needed to know, since Rick is good with firearms, he had a big range underground. This is about 3 feet under his house. I see why he live so far back in the woods, just like I said he has a lot to hide. I was there for hours counting money, making deals, testing product, conducting all type of business damn I know I'm a straight A student but this is a bit too much I have to suck it up and get the job done because I put everyone I love at risk and they don't even know what lies ahead and Lucky don't even know that my father's working for the FBI. Shit how is that going to look, I thought to myself I cannot ever tell Lucky this. I hoped that he would never find out because if his brother knows, he might think that I am an informant and kill my ass on the spot. Damn what am I going to do?

That night when I went home, I had so many thoughts running through my mind. I must be the best at what I do, I must pull this off, but my heart was beating a mile per minute. I kept telling myself girl get a grip you took acting in school even though this shit is real life, I am just playing a part, and I must do my best to play the part well. So, the next morning I got up like nothing happened, I looked in the mirror and stated to myself remember your just playing a part, I kept telling myself. So, as I was starting to get ready for school, my phone ring it was Lucky, Hi babe yes my love don't forget to keep your eyes open, don't trust no one and always keep your gun by your side and if anyone comes up to you asking about me just say you don't know me but keep your eyes on them and watch their hand movements. I will send Tony to keep an eye on you, only answer my calls just let the phone ring 3 times before you answer, ok babe.

CHAPTER NINE

I hung up and speaking in my inner voice how am I going to sneak this gun into school? I decided to put the gun under my skirt and strap it to my thigh, damn if anyone finds out I can be expelled from school and put in jail. To tell the truth at this point I do not care damn my life is at risk and I am going to do what I must do to stay alive. Man, today felt like the longest day of my life in school. Shit, I thought everyone was out to get me. I was nervous as hell at one point when my teacher looked at me some type of way, I said to myself if her hands move toward me in a strange way this bitch is going down.

I was so paranoid I was losing my mind behind this. Later that day my phone rang, I remember Lucky said let the phone ring three times, then answer it but it only ring once who could that be, because I did not recognize that number at all. So, I am preparing myself for anything at this point. Then Tony pulled up he said to me Alisha are you ready to go, Lucky said we must meet him back at the house so get in. Even though this is Lucky right-hand man, I remember what Lucky said trust only yourself.

So, if this dude even flinches a little, he will get a slug right between the eyes. When we arrived at the house Lucky said to me babe, we have a business meeting to attend to. I was preparing myself to go to war, if I must because Ricky said that I was mark for death too, so Lucky turned to me and said tonight is your big night. I want you to look your best wear something sexy and tight to capture everyone attention. I want all eyes on you tonight so be ready by eight oks. So, I started getting ready.

I have so many thoughts running through my head, like who are these people I am meeting, or I hope I do not have to test any product tonight. So, when 8 o'clock came I was dresses to impress. I kept telling myself that if no one noticed me tonight that they must be blind. We arrived at our destination and to my surprise it was an upscale club, it looked like anyone who is anyone was there. As we entered inside Lucky started introducing me to people that he knew then we went and sat at the bar, he told me that he will be right back. Lucky went into a room in the back of the club, the music was pumping so damn loud the song that the DJ was playing was turning me on. Then Lucky came back out of the back room, He told me to come here because he had some people that he would love for me meet, to my surprise the man that he introduces me to works with my father.

I remember seeing him twice before at my house. I was saying to myself shit I hope this man do not recognize me. I must play it off, but damn Lucky do not know that this ass hole is an FBI agent and he done sold his self to the devil. Oh my god oh my god we are going to get life for this shit. If Rick finds out about me, I am dead for sure.

My heart is racing right now, I am praying that Lucky do not introduce me by my real name Alisha to James who is the FBI agent that works with my father. The whole time I am saying to myself oh please oh please do not say my name, then Lucky turned around to James and said this is my Queen and I taught her everything I know. I was like oh damn he done rat me out now I am an accessory to all of his crimes, if he only knew he just gave me my death sentence, now I am an accomplice to everything that he has done. So, James turned around and held my hand and kiss it and said its and honor to meet you my Queen finally and cracked a smile and I said likewise. But in my thoughts, I am saying to myself I'm going to have to kill this man just in case he knows who I am, and I can't afford for anyone to find out about me and who's my father is. While we sat in the back room around the table discussing the business my eyes were on everyone and their hands, I was not taking my eyes off no one. Lucky did not even know that I had gun strap to my thighs under my dress. I came prepared this time if I am going down, I am damn sure taking a few out right along with me. During the meeting I was trying to figure out what was James doing here dealing with these types of people.

CHAPTER TEN

I am wondering is he undercover or is he a crooked agent. I am going to keep my eyes on him and to find out what he really wants. So that night the business meeting was a success, I made sure that I did not forget anyone face that was there at that meeting. I was taught memorize and recognize every face and voice when you are doing business. On our way home, I wanted to tell Lucky so bad that the guy he is doing business with it is not the person whom he thinks he is. If he knew that James was an FBI agent and I knew all along he would never forgive me and think that I was trying to set him up. Damn I love this man so much that I would even commit murder for him, man I am in too deep.

When I arrived home my father was pacing up and down, I was telling myself damn James done rat me out to my father and he is going to kill me for this. But on the other hand, If James is crooked my dad life could seriously be danger because he is working with a man that playing both sides and that type of person is extremely dangerous, so I asked my dad what's the matter? I never seen him this worried before, he said nothing baby girl for you to worried about. I got everything under control, so he gave me a kiss on the head and told me to get ready for bed. So, I decided to find out what is going on with him one way or the other. I knew that I should not be spying on my dad's private life but to ease my mind this is something that I must do because it looks like I am not the only one living a double life.

When my dad thought that everyone was fast asleep I decided to sneak downstairs I was walking so softly not to make a sound and I came across his dine and heard him on the phone talking in a secret code to this guy name Marolus Deserta, and I'm saying to myself that I heard that name before mention when Lucky was talking to his brother Rick, and Rick made a statement that were at war with the Deserta family after Lucky had killed that man. I know this could not be the same family if it is, is my father working for them I wonder, and the only thing I understood out of that whole conversation was kill Lucky and his bitch Queen. Oh my god I could not believe this, my father is after the man I love and myself. The saying is true do not go looking for things because you do not want to find out the answer. What am I am going to do, so I slowly walked back upstairs to my room, now I am going out of my mind?

I just cannot digest what I just heard. The man that I look up to and in my eyes, he could not do no wrong is a trader and turn coat. I cannot believe that all these years he been lying to the family, my poor mother this would just kill her or is she also involved in his corrupted ways. I better not find out that she was down with this to all along. I want to call Lucky and tell him so bad but I better wait and find out just exactly what he is up to and hearing him repeat kill the bitch Queen to, just messes my head up so I better watch my father more closely to because even though he's my father and don't get me wrong I love him but shit I will put a bullet in his head without no hesitation because he's setting out to kill me and Lucky and I'm not taking no prisoners alive and if my mom is down with it to she will meet the same fate as well just like my father.

At this point I do not trust no one. Everyone seems to be hiding secrets lately. The next morning I woke up like nothing happened I ran a nice hot bubble bath with my gun beside me on the floor underneath a towel, now that I know my father is out to kill me for the Deserta family, I can't let him catch me slipping if anyone try's to open the door or enter inside this bathroom all hell is going to break loose it will be a free for all up in this bitch, I knew that I was sounding a little crazy or maybe paranoid but I don't know whom to trust because I remember Rick said that I'm mark for death. And believe me I am taking this seriously. I am sitting here listening to every little sound that surrounds me. When I got out of the tub, I just threw the towel around me dripping wet and had my hand on my gun, you can never be too safe.

So, I opened the door then I check from left to right to see if anyone was coming so I did not hear or see if anyone, so I went into room and decided to make a survival plan. I put a chair up against the door and made damn sure, I lock myself inside while my bed facing the door, so no one can catch me off guard even though I know Tony is outside and my father don't even know Lucky have him guarding me and was ordering to take out anyone whom he felt was a threat to me. So, I left a night light on so that I can see my surroundings because everyone knows that shit always happens in the dark. So, I decided to get up early. I set my alarm for 7:00 to get an early start on everything and meet up with Lucky, because now I must really be on point.

CHAPTER ELEVEN

When it comes to firing my weapon, I am against the FBI and the Deserta family and I do not know who else. Little by little I am finding things out about everybody and they are not going to catch me slipping and have my back against the wall. Thinking about all of this got me beat I'm so tired, I feel if I close my eyes right now it will be hard for me to wake up but I'll take my chances because I was always told if you're tired and don't get enough rest you cannot think with a clear head and my head must be clear so that I can survive this outcome. So, I dimmed the lights in my room and fell asleep. Before I knew it, I started dreaming that someone was chasing me. I cannot see or recognize the face. I am running so fast in my dream until my alarm went off.

I woke up sweating like a pig and my heart was racing a mile per minute. I was saying to myself thank god that alarm went off he almost caught me. I jumped out of the bed, took a shower and got dressed so quickly so that I can see Lucky. A whole bunch commotion going on, So I got out of the car to find out what happened, and Lucky had told me that an informant told him that he heard that the FBI was tracking their every move. I took a deep breath and swallowed because I already knew because remember he was dealing with one that night at the club and James work with my father. I tried to act surprised like I did not know. Then Lucky turned to me and said get ready baby girl the shit is about to hit the fan.

He looks over at Tony and told him, find out whose tracking us and send some of your boys to get rid of them at any means necessary. I was saying to myself, damn one of these guys is my father but I really cannot say too much. Lucky called a surprise meeting, he wanted everyone to be present by 10 o'clock. I am like oh no, what is going to happen next? So, when 10 o'clock arrived we met up at this warehouse out in no man's lands to me, it looked kind of creepy. When we arrived there, I noticed so many cars on the scene it was unbelievable to me that, so many people are involved with this type of life style it seems like everyone is on Lucky payroll from lawyers, to judges, cop, doctors, you could imagine my face. I am like damn when he said everyone who is powerful have something to give to the cause.

He was right, they all love that fast money and the rich lifestyle he was not playing. When the meeting started you could hear a pin drop in this place. That place was so pack everyone had their eyes on Lucky, remember they are all on his payroll. Lucky stood up just like he did when he made that announcement to everyone that I was his Queen, this time he said we have a big problem out there the enemy has come to shut us down and we must stop them at all cost. You must keep your eyes and ears open to everyone around you, stay strapped at all times. Remember the big man is watching, mind your banking accounts and your spending lifestyle they could be tracking your every move. If you see something report it as soon as possible, watch your love ones very closely, they could be in danger and held for ransom after Lucky said that I heard a familiar voice that shook deep in my soul. I turned around and to my surprise it was James, how and the hell did his ass get here now? He is known what their planning, this bitch is going to be one step ahead of Lucky.

I am going to have to take this man out soon, he is becoming a pain in my ass seriously. As the meeting adjourns, everyone started to leave, and Rick pulled Lucky aside and said Lucky there will be a shipment coming in tonight on Bay Parkway and I need for you to pick it up for me. Lucky looked over at me and turned to Rick and said I cannot do it tonight. I need some quality time with my Queen; Rick was a little upset because it was for the business and all. But Rick could not give Lucky what I have, I got the good stuff what he calls his medicine. Lucky said to Rick let Tao and Tony go handle it because you have your right-hand man and I have mines to represent for us and James can tag along just in case they need some arm power around, they usually use James to put a man down.

But I am saying to myself he's committing all these murders as an FBI agent; something is definitely going on with him and I need to find out soon before all hell break loose and someone, I care for may die. Rick called the guys over Tao, Tony, and James and told them that the shipment of Kilos will be coming in at 11:50 p.m. tonight on Bay Parkway and he needs for them to pick it up, I've tried my best not to look directly at James incase he really do recognize me and rat me out. So, I told Lucky that I have to make a call and excused myself from the mix, because I've been noticing James staring at me like a pervert and he better be very careful because Lucky will have his eyes removed because of that. Lucky is very jealous, remember he said he would kill and die for me and I take his words very seriously. When I came back inside Lucky said let us go home baby girl and told Rick and everyone good night. On our way home Lucky kept kissing me and telling me that he loved me, and he cannot wait to make love to me.

I did not say a word like the cat had my tongue. I love hearing Lucky speak it turns me on. You know deep down inside I want him just as much as he wants me. When we arrived home, we could not keep our hands off each other, we started snatching each other's clothes off right at the door, this man got me whipped. People always said you can never forget your first and I'm telling you they are so right, as he carried me upstairs to the bedroom he laid me on the bed and turned on the shower and came back to finish taking my clothes off.

He picks me up and carried me into the shower, while the hot water ran down on our bodies, he began kissing me so passionately all over. The pleasure he was giving me, I thought my knees were going to buckle and I would fall straight out of the shower. I tell you he really knows how to please a woman good, as we continue to make love the phone rings. Lucky did not want to stop and answer it, so they left a voice message, and the message said the next business deal the big boss wants to meet with you personally. They describe him as a tall black man about 6 feet with dark brown hair with a gold tee and built like a body builder or a football player, when I heard that my heart stop. I said to myself oh shit that's my father their talking about and I remember that night when I overheard him talking to Morales Deserta, plus I heard him mention to kill me and Lucky, so he thought he was going to kill Lucky tonight good thing Lucky decided to come home with me, Lucky just saved his own life tonight.

But now that I know my father is getting closer to us, I am going to have to kill him before he kills us. When the next business deal goes down, I will most definitely be there, and my father is not going to see me coming remember I am my father's child and I also know the tricks of the trades. Now he became enemy #2 marks for death for death on my list. As we finished making love, Lucky did not pay any attention to the message that was on the answering machine, but I did, as we laid in the bed holding each other. Now I turned the words he said to me back on him, I said Lucky, I love you I will kill for you and I will die for you as the tears roll down my cheek, Lucky squeezed me tight and said don't worry baby girl nothing will ever come between us. I was saying to myself I hope he is right because I know my father, he will make sure he gets the job done and there is no stopping him until he finishes what he started. When he said he is going to kill us he means every word He said. When Lucky fell asleep holding me, I decided to get out of the bed and call my home girl Lisa, but I call her Pookie, she is the one that be covering for me while I am at Lucky's house. She's knows just what to say to my parents and they believe her cause she's a church girl, but if they only knew how she really was she drinks, and party and have more sex then me, so we both keep each other secrets.

CHAPTER TWELVE

So that night when I called her, I told her I need her to do me a big favor. I told her that someone is trying to hurt Lucky and myself included and I need her to cover for me for a few days until I get to the bottom of it, she told me don't worry she got my back. So, I snuck back in the bed with Lucky and fell asleep. So, everything was going great as usual just like it was before when we just met all the madness somehow had calmed down. Days, weeks and months went by and everything was going well. When I arrived home from school I opened the door to see my mom sitting on the sofa looking sad and confused so I asked her what was the matter, she said baby girl I just have a lot on my mine, so I asked her where was my father and she said that he left on a business trip that his job had sent him on. I was saying to myself business trip my ass he is going after me and my man. She stated that he will be gone for at least 4 days.

I gave her a kiss on the head and said to her, mom you know what type of work dad she says yes, and you know the risk he takes each and every day. What would you do if someone came and told you that he has been killed in the line of duty? Can you go on without him? She replied I knew what I was getting into when I married him and I prepared myself each and every day that there will be a knock on the door from the FBI telling me he was killed in the line of duty, so to answer your question, I'm already prepared. I told her I love you and then walked away. Now I have to get in touch with Lucky because I know my father out there plotting to kill both of us and if it's not him it will be the Deserta themselves, like I said before, this type of life leaves you in prison or death and I'm not trying to be a part of neither one. My phone started vibrating in my bag I answered, and it was Lucky, I said I was just going to call you what are you doing.

I need to see you, he said ok babe I have a business meeting to attend to, tonight and I will pick you up later, I said a business meeting with whom, remember the business deal that Rick setup before? Oh yeah, I remember so whose all going with you, he replied Tony and his boys, I ask is James going too and Lucky replied not this time he said, oh really I thought to myself is James and my father working together are they plotting against us? James already seen my face he knows I am Lucky Queen, but my father never seen Queen before, so I said to Lucky can I please go along even if I have to wait in the car until you finish. Remember you said I have to know the business and follow everything you do he said ok baby girl you got me on this one I'll send Tony to pick you up around 5 so that we can spend some time together before we go, I said yeah you right I don't know what might happen tonight. I'm coming to protect my man and myself even if I must take my father down, my mom is already prepared herself, so she doesn't even know she just gave me the green like to kill, so the time has come Lucky and I had a beautiful time together. I made sure of that because I do not know if we are going to make it out alive only god knows our faith. If anyone wondering I am scared hell yeah. I might be killed tonight but I am not going down without a fight man Lucky do not even know his faith like I do so since I can't tell him the truth, I must take matters in my own hands. Damn please do not let them catch me slipping, as we arrived at the meeting.

I was scoping out the place, my eyes were wide open I am checking out my surrounding not missing any details of where I am at. It's so quiet its creeping me out, you can't tell if someone going to jump out of know where and start shooting so I had my hand on my trigger just in case, like I was always told, always expected the unexpected. So, we have come to a full stop. The gate opened and two armed men escorted our cars through, but no one knew that I was there because I was hidden in the back seat and they just saw Lucky and his men. See remember I was not a part of this business deal and this deal was in an exclusive place, I'm like damn if shit breaks out you have to travel for miles to get help, good thing I hid an extra gun and ammunition under the seat before we got here, I snuck out of the house and hid it in the car while Lucky was getting dress. I'm not playing, this shit is real not like the stuff you see on TV I'm living it right now, so when everyone got out of their cars and greeted each other, things just didn't feel right or seem right either. Lucky was holding a brief case full of money, while Tony was standing beside him. I was observing every little detail from the car, and then suddenly, my father steps out of the vehicle my heart felt like it just stops and completely fell into my lap.

I was thinking to myself oh my god something is about to go down and I know for sure someone is not coming out of this deal alive. Then my father said you are Lucky I heard so much about you. I been waiting to see you and Miss Queen for quite some time, it would be an honor to meet her too. Lucky replied you will meet her sooner than you think. While they were talking Tony was testing the product, to make sure his ass was not selling them some bad shit because he learned his lesson from before with that deal with the Deserta family and now he's being extra cautious, but in a blink of an eye all hell broke loose. Tony tested the product and he turned around to Lucky, the expression on his face was priceless he did not even have to say a word it was written all over his face, the shit was no good. Tony reached for his magnum under his jacket and open fired, Lucky threw the brief case by the car and pulled out his gun. I was screaming watch out, it was total mayhem. Guns were going off like crazy, rounds were flying over the car. I grabbed the saw off shot gun from under the seat.

I opened the door and fell to the ground I heard Lucky telling his boys to run it is a setup. I picked up the briefcase with the money inside. I was hiding beside the car, no one knew that I was there. So, I opened fire on the crowd where Lucky and his boys was being ambushed, they did not know where the rounds were coming from. All I kept thinking was someone I love is going to die, God please protect us and forgive me for what I am about to do. Either I am going to make it out alive or be killed but at least I said my goodbyes to my mother. Then I heard Lucky yell out oh no Tony's been hit.

I could not think straight, something just came over me. I became heartless; I just started shooting at anything that moved. It was so freaking dark and I knew either my father or James and the Deserta family was hunting for blood and they were going to make damn sure no one was coming out alive. Like they said money is the root of all evils. I heard two voices that sounded so familiar. Is that James and Rick I hear? What and the hell are they doing here? This shit is getting crazy it going from bad to worst are they plotting against us, I caught up to Lucky and saw him holding Tony, I said Lucky what's your brother and James doing here, he said what? I said I heard them back there did he know about this deal? And where the meeting was being held? He said no. So, why are they here Lucky? Are they trying to kill us? Like I told you before and I told your brother I love you I will kill for you and I will die for you and I mean it. If your brother is a part of it Lucky, I will kill him. Lucky turned around and looked at me and said Queen we are going to have to kill to make it out alive.

So, I said to Lucky do you trust me with your life he said yes. I have something to tell you please just listen and do not say a word until I am finish. That man you were doing the deal with at the club your brother right hand man James is an FBI agent and the deal that went bad tonight that man is my father. I could not tell you, I thought if you knew you would leave me or even kill me. I am in too deep into this relationship and I love you more than life itself. Now that you know, would you stand by my side? Would you ride or die for me like I did for you? When I told him, it looked like all the blood drain out of Lucky face. I was surprised with what he said to me when he opened his mouth, he said kill everything I mean everything that moves, including your father and my brother plus James. If you get a clear shot do not hesitate to fire. Let's take them down, he laid Tony in a corner while he was bleeding he said to Tony I'm not going to let you die, Lucky turned around to me and said are you ready I answer yes. This is war we took off in different directions to corner them and the first one I came in contact with was James. He's very good in killing so I ran up on him and opened fired right to the head and kept it moving I didn't even wait to see the body drop, I was saying to myself one down and more to go.

I should have known that Rick was a part of this because one he is jealous of Lucky and his power over the people and Lucy lifestyle. He is mad that Lucky did not let him handle the situation with the Deserta family, so all along he was working with them to bring Lucky empire down and even kill him. I warned Rick when we first met if anyone tries to come between us, I will kill them, and he is no different from my father. He better prays that I do not catch him slipping because he will meet the same fate as the others, and I will not stop until I get the job done remember I am my father child. So, they better pray that Lucky catches them first. While the guns were still blazing, I am running in the dark. I stopped in my tracks to hear everything around me, just like Lucky said listen and observed your surroundings and perceive with caution because for one my father and Rick are very skillful they both are excellent sharp shooters and James was better than the both of them and I took him out with one shot. He got caught slipping and never seen me coming remember no one knew I was there. Even though I had blood on my clothes it will be plenty more before the night is over which you can count on that, I am not leaving any witnesses behind to point a finger at me. But I cannot take anything for granted at this point, all of sudden I heard a big explosion and seen flames starting to surround me. I thought to myself they are trying to smoke us out but if I want to come out of this alive, I must play it smart and always be one step ahead.

I must find Lucky because it is so damn dark out here, they could have had night vision glasses and could have been watching me at that moment. So, I ran in between two crates and decided to text Lucky to see where he is at but was not getting any answer. I am worried now, I hoped he did not get caught because my father wants him dead more than anything right now. When I looked up, I saw a shadow run right pass me, I bend down so the person could not see me. I did not know who it was, but I was damn sure going to find out. So, I got down to the floor and started crawling on my hands and knees trying not to make a sound because if it's one of my enemies he will sure enough shoot me down without any hesitation because now it's us against them.

While I was on my knees looking through the cracks between the crates trying to see if I could identify if he were one of the enemies. Damn it is so dark and the smog from the smoke is unbearable, it is so hard to see and breath. Man, I hope I do not pass out. I wanted to use the flashlight on my phone, but I knew if anyone seen where the lights were coming from, I knew I was dead for sure, if it was one of our enemies. Why won't Lucky text me to let me know if he is ok? Shit I am about to go crazy not knowing if my people are dead or alive. I got to get a grip I heard someone coming up behind me and it was Rick. He did not see me because I was hiding in between the two crates, if I could only get a clear shot, I would have taken him down. I will get another chance at it hopefully. I wished Lucky would get in contact with me and let me know that he was ok. I was also worried about Tony, if we do not get out of here soon, he is going to bleed to death.

I am sitting here on the floor reminiscing about how our relationship began. I never knew when I woke up that morning that might be my last day on earth. Then in an instant I heard a loud yell and shots fired. I thought to myself please do not let it be Lucky because he was not answering my text. I emerged from behind the crates to find Lucky and to follow where the sound came from. I approached and I saw my father with a gun in his hand aiming at someone on the ground and I creeped a little closer and I notice he was aiming at Lucky. My man face was battered and bruised but my father was so focused on Lucky that he did not hear or see me coming. I had my gun in my hand with my finger on the trigger and I came for blood, but I had to approach my father right because one false move he would end the love of my life without any hesitation. When I kill my father, I want him to see my face and I want him to see my eyes and let him know whose killing him. He must have snuck up on Lucky to capture him, so I took a deep breath because this was my father, this is the man I worship and looked up too and loved for so many years. Now it comes down to this his life or mines and Lucky and I chose us.

As I walked up behind him, I said Hi father. I startled him as he turned around. I had my gun aimed at his head and he had his gun aimed at Lucky's chest. He said what are you doing here? I said that is the same question I would like to know too. What happen to the man I loved and admired so much? He said, what happened to my baby girl the love of my life? I said I grew up. You said you wanted to meet that bitch that they called Queen so father here I am. Your little girl is no more, and I kept my eyes on him at all times because I knew my father, he is good at what he does. Like they said I am my father's child, you do not remember Lucky told you that you would meet Queen sooner than you know and I am here standing right in front you. I love that man that you have beaten and tortured, and I am not leaving here without him. Then my father said to me baby girl you do not know what you have gotten yourself into. I love you, but a job is a job and if I must kill you too so be it. Oh, what the fuck old man, you are not the only one with skills it looks like mom will not have two coming home for dinner. Then I heard a noise coming up behind me it was Rick, he had his gun aimed at the back of my head and he knew if he shot me my gun is going to go off and kill my father. He did not want that to happened because my father is the Deserta family right hand man and if anything should happen to my father because of him, they would kill Rick's entire family. Lucky looked over at Rick and said Rick what happened between us? He said you know what happened you choose that bitch over me and she must go. At that moment shot was fired, Rick fell to the floor. Where did that shot come from? It was Tony, Lucky crawled over to Tony to help him. Tony told Lucky before he passed out, I told you that I would protect Queen with my life.

While Rick was lying on the floor bleeding and yelling for Lucky to help him. Lucky picked up Tony's gun and walked over to Rick and said Rick I love bro and I always will, but I told you that I would kill and die for my Queen. You tried to take her from me so now you see I am my brother's keeper and shot Rick right in his head. I still had my gun aimed at my father head and said I love you father till death do us part, then I heard a shot fired and I passed out on the floor. I could hear voices all around me, but I just could not get myself to wake up, even though I could hear Lucky calling my name, but I just could not answer. I felt a cold chill coming across me and I wanted to yell out. It felt like someone was holding my mouth shut. I was trying to figure out what in the hell was going on. Was I shot? or did I shoot my father and because I was so frightened that I passed out. God please help me; damn it almost feels like I am in a trance. Please let me wake up. I need to know what happened. I need to be with my man. What is going on? Can anyone hear me? Am I dead? I felt so cold, I seen a bright light. Is someone shining a light in my face? I am starting to feel scared help me babe, I need to feel you beside me. You promised you would never let nothing, or no one ever hurt me. Just in a matter of seconds, I heard Lucky call out to me Queen! Then silence was all I heard then the light that was shining in my face turned dark. Wait!

Made in the USA
Columbia, SC
26 October 2020